SPEEDWAY PUBLIC LIBRARY
3 5550 430

D1409490

SOCCER 'CATS

#11

Making the Save

Matt Christopher®

Text by Stephanie Peters

Illustrated by Daniel Vasconcellos

LITTLE, BROWN AND COMPANY
New York Boston

Little, Brown and Company

Time Warner Book Group
1271 Avenue of the Americas, New York, NY 10020
Visit our Web site at www.lb-kids.com

First Edition

Library of Congress Cataloging-in-Publication Data

Peters, Stephanie True.
Making the save / Matt Christopher ; text by Stephanie Peters ; illustrated by Daniel Vasconcellos.—1st ed.
p. cm.—(Soccer 'cats ; #11)
Summary: When the Soccer 'Cats decide to earn money to buy a gift for Coach Bradley, Bucky goes out of his way to make the gift a wonderful surprise.
ISBN 0-316-73744-5 (hc)—ISBN 0-316-73745-3 (pb)
[1. Soccer—Fiction. 2. Gifts—Fiction. 3. Moneymaking projects—Fiction.] I. Vasconcellos, Daniel, ill. II. Title. III. Series: Christopher, Matt. Soccer Cats ; v #11.
PZ7.P441833Mak 2004
[Fic]—dc22 2003020201

10 9 8 7 6 5 4 3 2 1

WOR/CWO

Printed in the United States of America

Soccer 'Cats Team Roster

Lou Barnes	*Striker*
Jerry Dinh	*Striker*
Stookie Norris	*Striker*
Dewey London	*Halfback*
Bundy Neel	*Halfback*
Amanda Caler	*Halfback*
Brant Davis	*Fullback*
Lisa Gaddy	*Fullback*
Ted Gaddy	*Fullback*
Alan Minter	*Fullback*
Bucky Pinter	*Goalie*

Subs:

Jason Shearer

Dale Tuget

Roy Boswick

Edith "Eddie" Sweeny

Chapter 1

Thwap! Bucky Pinter slapped down the soccer ball Dewey London kicked at him. He sent the ball rolling back to Dewey. Dewey trapped it with his foot, lined up behind it, and kicked again. This time, Bucky jumped high to tap the ball up and over the goal.

"Another great save, Bucky!" Dewey cried enthusiastically.

Bucky retrieved the ball. "Thanks for practicing with me today," he said. "I want to be sure I'm ready for our last game!" Bucky was the starting goalkeeper for the Soccer 'Cats. Dewey played halfback.

"It'd be awesome to end the season with a win," Dewey agreed. He punted the ball at Bucky.

It was a soft kick, and Bucky caught it easily. This time, instead of sending the ball back to Dewey, he started bouncing it from knee to knee. "I've been thinking," he said. "Maybe we should get Coach Bradley a thank-you present for all he's done for our team. What do you think?"

Dewey nodded. "Sounds good to me. Let's talk to Bundy and see what he thinks. He is the captain of the team, after all." He checked his watch. "Bundy had a dentist appointment earlier, but he should be home by now. Want to head over to his house?"

Bucky gave the ball one last bounce. "Sure. Think his mom will feed us lunch? I'm starving!"

Several minutes later, the two boys were

sitting with Bundy at his kitchen table. Bucky and Dewey were eating sandwiches and chips. Bundy had a bowl of applesauce.

"Is that all you're having for lunch?" Dewey asked, his mouth full of peanut butter and jelly.

"I can't chew. My lips and tongue are numb," Bundy replied. At least that's what Bucky thought he said. It sounded more like, "Ah cad tsew. By libs ad tug ah nub."

Mrs. Neel explained, "Bundy had a cavity. The dentist gave him a shot to numb the area around the tooth so he could drill out the cavity without hurting Bundy. The numb feeling will wear off in a while."

Dewey looked horrified. "A shot? Did it hurt?" Bundy nodded miserably.

His mother kissed the top of his head. "It'll feel better soon. And maybe now you'll stay away from sugary snacks and drinks!"

Bucky watched Bundy scoop up a spoonful of applesauce and carefully put it in his mouth. He decided to follow Mrs. Neel's advice. He sure didn't want to have to get a shot in his mouth!

As the three boys ate their lunches, Bucky brought up his idea. "So, what do you think, Captain Bundy? Should we get the coach a thank-you present?"

Bundy nodded. He opened his mouth to say something, but before he could speak, his mother interrupted. "I think it would be a great idea. I just have two questions." She turned from the counter and looked at the three boys. "First: What are you going to get him? And second: How are you going to pay for it?"

Chapter 2

Bucky gulped. He had an idea for the present, but he hadn't really given much thought to where the money would come from.

Mrs. Neel seemed to realize that. "I suppose we, your parents, could just give you the money," she said. "But then the gift wouldn't really be from you and your teammates, would it?"

"So we need to figure out a way to earn the money ourselves," Dewey finished for her. "Maybe we could have a bake sale. You know, make cookies and cakes and sell 'em to people?"

Bundy shook his head violently. "No way!" he said, his speech still a little garbled. "I'm staying away from sugar!"

"A lemonade stand?" Dewey smacked his lips. "I love lemonade!"

The other two boys shook their heads. "Lemonade stands are for little kids," Bundy said. "Besides, no one ever makes money from them. Why don't we just ask everyone to break open their piggy banks? I bet I've got a couple of dollars in mine."

"We could," Bucky agreed. "But I think it'd be better to come up with a way to earn money as a team."

The three boys were quiet for a few minutes, each trying to think up a way to make money. Then Bucky snapped his fingers. "I've got it!" he cried. "How about a car wash?"

"A car wash?" Dewey looked doubtful. "How would we do that?"

"Easy!" replied Bucky. "We'll get buckets and sponges and towels. We fill the buckets with warm, soapy water. A car drives up, we wash it with the soapy water, and we collect the money!"

"Where does the car drive up? And how do we get the car rinsed off?" Bundy asked.

But by now Bucky had it all figured out. "We'll have it at my house since I live on a dead-end street and cars can park without blocking traffic. We've got a long hose we can use to spray off the soap. We can even towel dry the cars after they're clean." He grinned. "So, what do you think?"

"I think a lemonade stand would be easier," Dewey said. "Tastier, too."

Bucky laughed. "Then we'll also set up a lemonade stand and make twice as much money!"

Bundy stood up. "Let's call a team meeting and see what everyone else thinks." Suddenly, he blinked. "Hey, I can feel my tongue and lips again!"

Bucky grabbed the phone. "Just in the nick of time," he said. "Start making those calls!"

Within an hour, the whole team had gathered in Bundy's backyard. Once more, Bucky explained his idea about getting the coach a gift. He outlined the plan for the car wash, too. When he was through, everyone began talking at once.

"I'll make some signs to put up around town," Amanda Caler offered.

"My dad's got this stuff that makes hubcaps shine like new," said Brant Davis. "I'll see if I can bring it."

"I don't like lemonade," muttered Stookie Norris, not bothering to look up from the handheld computer game he was playing. The game was Stookie's prize possession. He never went anywhere without it.

"More for the rest of us, then!" Jason Shearer said.

"But only if you pay for it," Bundy reminded them.

"That's right," agreed Bucky. "We need to make a lot of money to cover the cost of the present I found!"

Chapter 3

Stookie looked up and frowned. "Hold on. You already bought the present?" he asked.

"No, no," Bucky reassured him.

"Good," said Stookie, "because I think we should get him—"

Bucky interrupted. "I'm sure your idea is good, Stookie, but let me tell you about mine!" He turned to the others. "I saw this wool-and-leather jacket in the window of Rocko's Sporting Goods. It looked like the team jackets some professional athletes wear—you know, the kind that snap up the front?"

A few of the kids nodded. "It comes in different colors, including yellow like our team T-shirt."

"You want to get him a yellow jacket?" Jason grinned. "Heck, why not go all out and get him a whole bees' nest instead?"

Bucky laughed with the others, then continued. "The jacket was pretty cool-looking, but the best part is, we can get words and stuff stitched on it. For *free*."

"What would we put on it?" Edith "Eddie" Sweeny wanted to know.

"I was thinking something like 'World's Best Coach' and our team logo."

"How much does it cost?" Amanda asked.

Bucky told his teammates the price he'd seen on the tag. The twins, Ted and Lisa Gaddy, whistled at the same time.

"That's a lot!" Lisa said.

"A real lot!" Ted echoed.

"Well, I think Coach Bradley is worth it." Bundy's words stopped anyone else from commenting. "I say we try to earn the money for the jacket. If we raise enough, great! If not"— he shrugged—"I bet we can find something else just as good."

"Don't we get to vote on it?" Stookie said. "Or is it whatever Bucky says goes?"

"Sure, we can vote," Bundy said. "All in favor?" Everyone but Stookie raised a hand. "Sorry, Stookie, looks like you're the odd man out." Stookie didn't say a word. He just picked up his computer game and started playing again.

Bundy said, "Today's Monday. We have a practice tomorrow morning, and our last game is on Saturday. I think we should have the car wash on Wednesday. Okay?"

Stookie was silent, but everyone else agreed. Bucky ran inside to call his mother to make sure it was okay to have the car wash at their house. When he returned, he gave the team the thumbs-up.

"I'm going home right now to make the signs," Amanda said. "I've got tons of art supplies and cardboard."

"I'll help you," Lisa offered. "Then we can put them up today!"

"I'll come, too," Eddie said. The three girls hopped on their bikes and took off.

"Anyone want to help me make the lemonade stand?" Dewey asked. Lou Barnes and Jerry Dinh volunteered.

"C'mon, Alan." Jason grabbed Alan Minter's arm and pulled him along. "Let's go find some lemons." Alan followed him out of the yard. That left Bucky, Bundy, and Stookie.

"Wanna start rounding up some buckets?" Bundy asked. Bucky nodded, but Stookie rolled his eyes.

"I gotta get going," he said, pocketing his game. "See you at practice tomorrow." He threw a leg over his bike and disappeared around the corner.

"That Stookie," Bundy said. "He can be such a spoilsport."

"Yeah," Bucky said. "He's a really good player and all. But you know what? I sometimes hope we're not on the same team next year."

Chapter 4

That night, Bucky lay in bed listening to a light rain on the roof and imagining the coach taking the jacket out of the gift box and slipping it on.

Suddenly, Bucky sat up. *What if it doesn't fit?* he thought frantically. He flopped back down to think about the problem. As his head hit the pillow, the tag on his pajama top scratched his neck. His mother usually cut off the tags, but she had forgotten this time. The night was hot, so Bucky decided to sleep without his shirt. He struggled out of it and started to toss it on the floor. Then he stopped.

The tag! he thought happily, staring at his pajama top. *That's it!* He snuggled back into his bed. Tomorrow, if he was clever, he could find the answer he needed.

After the night's rain, the next morning turned out to be warm and sunny. Bucky showed up at the field a few minutes early. Coach Bradley was already there setting up two long lines of orange cones on the field. Bucky put his plan into action right away.

"Hey, Coach!" Bucky called. "Phew, it sure is a hot one today! I might just practice without my shirt on! How about you?"

The coach shrugged. "I'll keep mine on. And unless you're wearing sunscreen, don't take yours off, okay? I can't have my star goalkeeper getting a burn before our last game."

"Oh. Right," Bucky said. *Rats,* he thought.

The rest of the team slowly trickled in.

Coach Bradley had them all do warm-up exercises, then he separated them into two groups and explained their first drill.

"Bucky, you go in one goal, and Jason, you take the other. Group one, you're with Bucky, and two, with Jason." The kids followed the coach's instructions. "Two people from each group, take up positions near the goals." Dewey and Amanda trotted down near Bucky. Eddie and Lisa went to the opposite goal. "Now, everyone else line up behind the cones. First in line, dribble in and out of the cones. At the end, pass to one of the players near the goal. That player shoots on goal, then goes to the end of the line. The dribbler takes his or her place." He clapped his hands. "We're working on control and quickness. Ready? Go!"

Bucky crouched down, hands in the classic W goalkeeper's pose, ready to stop the ball when it came toward him. Stookie Norris dribbled expertly through the cones, then passed to Amanda. Amanda fired a shot to

the upper left corner of the goal. Bucky smacked the ball away and returned to his starting position. Amanda trotted to the end of the line, and Stookie took her place near the goal.

Next in line was Lou Barnes. Lou dribbled around the cones and booted the ball to Dewey. Dewey kicked it hard toward Bucky's feet. Bucky scooped up the ball and threw it to one side.

Ten minutes later, when the coach blew his whistle, Bucky was breathing hard and his shirt was covered with mud and grass. Looking down at himself, he suddenly had an idea. While the others were busy getting cups of water, Bucky quietly rolled a soccer ball in a muddy patch of grass.

"Hey, Coach!" he yelled. Coach Bradley turned—and Bucky fired the ball directly at his chest. "Catch!"

Chapter 5

"What the—*oof!*" The mud-covered soccer ball bounced off the coach's stomach and fell to the ground. Coach Bradley looked from his shirt to Bucky and back to his shirt. With a sigh, he picked up a towel and started wiping the mud off. "This shirt is as dirty as my van! If I don't get them both clean, Mrs. Bradley will have my head!"

"I know where you can get your van cleaned!" Stookie piped up.

"You do? Where?" the coach asked. Stookie shot Bucky a sly grin.

Bucky's eyes widened. *Was Stookie going to tell him about the car wash?*

He couldn't still be angry that Bucky had come up with the idea for the present—could he? One glance at Stookie told Bucky he was. *I've got to do something!* Bucky thought desperately. He spied a cup of water in Dewey's hands. Without thinking, he grabbed the cup and tossed it at the coach.

"Bucky!" Coach Bradley sputtered. "What's gotten into you?"

"I—I was just trying to help clean your shirt," Bucky said weakly.

The coach mopped his dripping face with the towel. Then he peeled off his wet shirt, tossed it on the bench, and started rummaging around in his duffel bag for a spare.

Quick as a wink, Bucky grabbed the muddy shirt. He pulled the tag out of the shirt's collar, examined it, and grinned. "Got it!"

"Yes, you do," the coach said. He held out his hand. "Now, may I please have it?"

With a sheepish grin, Bucky passed him the shirt. "Ready for that next drill whenever you are, Coach!"

Coach Bradley shook his head, then stuffed his dirty shirt into the duffel bag and faced the rest of the team. "Okay then," he barked. "Four-on-four scrimmage with goalies. We've got eleven kids here today. Whoever's left over, be ready to sub in. Let's get to it!"

Bucky jogged to his spot. Ted and Alan took up defensive positions near him, with Stookie and Eddie on offense. Playing offense for the other team were Lou and the other starting striker, Jerry Dinh. Jerry had the ball. At the coach's whistle, he started dribbling down the field. Ted and Alan immediately moved to double-team him. Jerry passed to Lou, then spun to free himself from Ted and Alan. "Here!" he called to Lou. Lou jabbed a pass to him, but the ball took a crazy bounce and wound up right in front of Ted. Ted knocked it over the sideline.

"Nice move, Jerry. Good 'D,' Ted," the coach called. "Lou, try to make those passes a little sharper, okay?"

Lou nodded and returned to his position. This time, he started with the ball. A fast runner, he streaked down the sideline and into firing range before Ted or Alan could reach him. One short shot later, the ball was in the net behind Bucky.

"Hmm, that's better, Lou!" Coach Bradley said with a smile. He tossed the ball to Stookie. "Do that during our last game, and we're sure to give the other team a run for their money!"

Just then, Stookie dribbled up next to the coach. "Speaking of money," he said, "I hear a great way to make some extra cash is to hold a car—*umph!*"

Bucky shot out of the goal and tackled him.

"Bucky!" Coach Bradley yelled. "What are you doing?"

Bucky stood up and helped Stookie to his feet. "Uh, sorry, Coach," he apologized. "I thought Stookie was going to take a shot. I was going for the ball. Sorry, Stookie."

Stookie curled his hands into fists. "Oh, you'll be sorry all right!"

"That's enough," Coach Bradley said, standing between the two boys. "I don't know what's going on here, but let's cool it. Stookie, back to your position." Stookie glared at Bucky but did as the coach asked.

"And Bucky, I don't know what's gotten into you today," the coach continued. "But I will tell you that if you don't settle down, I'm going to bench you at the start of the next game."

Chapter 6

Bucky couldn't believe his ears. Benched for the 'Cats' last game? He just couldn't be!

This is all Stookie's fault, he thought angrily. *He's trying to ruin everything!*

The scrimmage continued, but Bucky was so worried about being benched that he couldn't focus on goalkeeping. One ball after another flew by him and into the net. Finally, Coach Bradley blew his whistle to end the drill.

"Okay, that's it for today," the coach called. "Gather up the cones and the balls, please, and bring them to my van."

Bucky helped the others collect the equipment. He kept a close eye on Stookie the whole time, ready to intervene if he started telling the coach about the car wash again. Stookie didn't. Still, Bucky relaxed only after he saw Stookie climb into his mother's car and drive away.

Bucky's mother hadn't arrived yet, so he helped the coach load the remaining equipment into the van. The coach slammed the back shut, then looked at his hands and grimaced. "My van really is filthy." He wiped his hands on a towel. "I gotta find a car wash."

Bucky's mouth turned dry. What if the coach saw the signs Amanda, Eddie, and Lisa had put up?

"Take them down! All of them!" Bucky yelled into the phone that night.

"What are you talking about?" He could hear the confusion in Amanda's voice.

"If the coach sees the signs, he'll go to the

CAR WASH

car wash tomorrow!" Bucky explained desperately. "So we have to take them down!"

"But Bucky," Amanda said, "if we take them down, no one else will know about the car wash!"

Bucky groaned. "Shoot, you're right! What are we going to do?"

He heard Amanda sigh. "I think there's only one thing we can do—hope the coach got his car washed today or is too busy to do it tomorrow."

Bucky felt his heart leap. "Amanda, that's it! You're a genius!"

"I am? What—"

"I can't talk now," Bucky said hurriedly. "Leave the signs up. Bye!" He hung up on Amanda and punched in a new number. "Please be home," he muttered as the phone rang on the other end.

"Hello?" a deep voice answered.

"Coach Bradley? Bucky here," Bucky squeaked nervously. "I need your help!"

"What can I do for you?" The coach sounded surprised.

"I think I've lost my touch," Bucky lied. "I'm afraid the other team is going to score like crazy on me unless I get in some extra practice."

"Well, why don't you see if some of your teammates can take shots on you tomorrow?"

"No!" Bucky yelled. "I mean, I need your expert advice. Please, Coach?"

The coach was silent. "Okay," he finally said. "I could come over Thursday—"

"It has to be tomorrow morning at ten o'clock," Bucky cut in. "And we have to meet at the field, not here." He held his breath. Had he pushed too far?

To his relief, Coach Bradley started laughing. "Okay. See you at the field tomorrow." He hung up.

Bucky hung up, too. Then he called Bundy to explain why he wouldn't be at the car wash the next day.

Chapter 7

Bucky was at the field ten minutes to ten the next morning. Coach Bradley arrived at ten o'clock on the dot. He parked the van and joined Bucky.

"Hey, Coach," Bucky said. "Thanks again for helping me out."

Coach Bradley tossed a few soccer balls onto the field in front of the goal. "No problem," he said. "I can only stay for a little while, though. Then I have to get some errands done."

"Errands? What errands?" Bucky asked. He

glanced at the van. To his dismay, he saw it was still covered with dirt.

"Oh, just some stuff," the coach answered vaguely. "Nothing urgent, but they need to be done today. Well, let's get started." He strode off toward the goal.

Bucky followed. *Two hours,* he thought. *I just have to keep him busy for two hours.*

"We'll begin with our usual warm-up. I'll kick the ball, you catch it or slap it out of the way. All set?"

Bucky nodded and got into ready position. Coach Bradley lined up behind a ball. He gave it an easy kick, lobbing toward Bucky's right side at shoulder height. Instinctively, Bucky reached up and caught the ball.

"Good, no problems there!" The coach smiled encouragingly.

Bucky smiled, too. But as he rolled the ball back to the coach, he wanted to kick himself. *I've got to mess up or else this practice will be over before it's begun!* he thought.

With this in mind, he got ready for the next kick. It came as a soft shot to the corner. One quick side step, and Bucky could be between the ball and the net. He'd done it a million times without a problem. But this time, as he stepped sideways, he tripped. He hit the dirt, and the ball rolled past him.

"Whoops!" said the coach. "You okay, Bucky?"

Bucky stood and brushed the dirt from his shirt. "Guess I'm a little clumsy today," he said.

The coach shrugged. "Well, let's try another."

Bucky flubbed the next one. And the next, and the next, and the next. After twenty minutes of missing balls, colliding with goal posts, and tripping over his own feet, Bucky was starting to feel a little foolish. Still, he was determined to keep up the act as long as Coach Bradley stayed with him.

Finally, however, the coach stopped the drill. "Bucky," he said, narrowing his eyes, "if

I didn't know any better, I'd say you were missing these balls on purpose."

Bucky tried to look innocent. "No way, Coach!" he protested. "I mean, why would I do something like that?"

"I don't know. But I will tell you this: Unless I see some pretty quick improvement, I'm going to have to start Jason in the goal our last game."

Bucky gulped. Suddenly, his plan to keep the coach busy didn't seem so smart anymore!

Chapter 8

Bucky risked a look at his watch. It was quarter after eleven. He had to keep the coach busy for at least another half hour! But he didn't dare continue to mess up. Playing goalie for the team's final game was too important to him. He decided to flub his saves every third time instead of every time.

He put his plan into action. Catch, save—miss. Catch, save—miss. Everything seemed to be going fine until—

"Bucky, are you playing some sort of game here?" The coach looked a little upset. "Or are you following a pattern of saves and misses because you think it's funny?"

Bucky didn't know what to say. He peeked at his watch again. Still fifteen minutes to go!

The coach checked his watch, too. Then he started to gather up the balls.

"Where—where are you going?" Bucky asked fearfully.

"I don't think more practice is going to change the way you're playing today, do you?" the coach replied. "Now, if you'll excuse me, I've got to be someplace by noon." He shoved the balls into a big mesh bag and started toward his van.

Bucky's mind spun frantically. The car wash ended at noon. Was that where the coach needed to be?

Maybe I should pretend to hurt myself, he thought. But he realized that idea wouldn't work. The coach wasn't dumb. He'd see right away that Bucky was faking it.

I'll ask him how he got interested in soccer,

Bucky decided. *Grown-ups always like to talk about themselves!*

He planted himself by the driver side of the van, blocking the door so the coach couldn't open it. "Say, Coach, I've been wondering," he said. "When did you first play soccer? What position did you play? Did you play for school teams? What was your team name? What—"

Coach Bradley cut him off. "Bucky, I'd be happy to answer all your questions." He reached over and gently moved Bucky away from the door. "But right now, I have to be going." He opened the van door, climbed inside, and started the engine. "I'll see you at the game on Saturday."

"But, Coach!" Bucky cried over the sound of the motor.

Coach Bradley smiled. "See you Saturday!" he called as he drove off.

Bucky hopped on his bike and pedaled as fast as he could, hoping to see where the coach was going. But by the time he reached the end of the parking lot, the van had disappeared. Bucky sighed and headed for home.

When he rounded the corner onto his dead-end street, he was relieved to see no sign of the coach's van. However, judging from the pile of money on the lemonade stand, many other cars and vans had been by.

A few teammates watched as Bundy and Dewey counted the money. Others were picking up buckets and sponges and gathering towels. As Bucky waved to his friends, he noticed that Stookie wasn't among them. He parked his bike next to the stand.

"Well?" he asked. "How'd we do?"

Bundy looked at Dewey. Dewey shook his head. "We don't have enough," he said. "Sorry, Bucky."

Chapter 9

Bucky couldn't believe it. All their hard work, all he'd risked by pretending to play badly and acting weird around the coach—all for nothing!

"Well," he said with a sigh, "at least we have enough to get him something, right?" He tried to hide his disappointment but failed. He'd been so looking forward to seeing the coach's expression when they gave him that jacket.

Most of them, anyway. Bucky felt his disappointment turn to anger when he thought of

Stookie. One thing was for sure—Stookie's name wouldn't be on the card they put with the present!

Bucky was just about to say as much to his friends, when Stookie himself rode up on his bike. Bucky put his hands on his hips, waiting for Stookie to start gloating over their failure. But to his surprise, Stookie looked anything but smug. Unbelievably, he looked sort of ashamed!

"Hi, guys," he said in a low voice. "Sorry I missed the car wash. And sorry I've been acting like an idiot. Sometimes I let my temper get out of control, you know? But the team is what matters now, so if it's not too late, I'd like to make a donation to the present fund." He drew a wad of bills out of his pocket and handed them to Dewey. Dewey's eyes widened.

"What bank did you rob to get this much money?" he asked.

"No bank," Stookie said. "I—I just sold something." He wouldn't say anything else.

COACH

"We've got enough money! What are we waiting for?" Bundy yelled. "Let's head to Rocko's right now!"

The jacket was ready by Friday night. Bucky wrapped it in special soccer paper. He taped the card that everyone—including Stookie—had signed to the outside of the package. He put the present on the nightstand next to his bed and fell asleep with one hand resting on it.

The next morning was a perfect soccer day—warm, but not too warm, cloudy, but with just enough sun to make people feel cheerful. Bundy hid the present under the bench. They were going to give it to the coach after the game.

After warm-ups, the coach called out the starting roster. As usual, Lou, Stookie, and Jerry were starting as the strikers. At the half-back positions were Amanda, Bundy, and Dewey. Brant, Lisa, Alan, and Ted were the fullbacks.

"And in the goal, let's have Bucky," the coach finished. Bucky's breath came out in a *whoosh.* Coach Bradley gave him a wink. "Feeling up to it today, Bucky?" he asked.

"Absolutely, sir!" Bucky replied.

The 'Cats were playing the Torpedoes, the toughest team in the league. The 'Cats had won a few and lost a few to the Torpedoes. Today, they hoped to add one last win. They knew the Torpedoes were hoping to do the same.

The 'Cats won the coin toss and started out with the ball. At the ref's whistle, Stookie toed the ball to Jerry, then dashed downfield, looking for a pass. Jerry dribbled quickly down the sideline. Two Torpedoes jumped in front of him, stabbing at the ball with their feet. Jerry worked to keep control, but the ball bounced over the sideline.

Amanda threw the ball in. She aimed for Jerry, but a Torpedo halfback stole the ball. Before Jerry could stop her, the Torpedo was off and running toward the 'Cats goal. Amanda rushed to interfere. The Torpedo booted the ball to her center striker. He dribbled it down the field like a pro, dodged past Bundy, and tricked Ted with a fake. Suddenly, he was right in front of Bucky!

Chapter 10

The Torpedo kicked the ball high to the right corner. Bucky leaped sideways, arms outstretched—and just managed to tap the ball up and over the goal! Shouts of joy mingled with cries of disappointment.

The ref retrieved the ball and set it in the corner circle for a corner kick. Players from both teams crowded near the goal. Bucky crouched down, ready and waiting. The Torpedo launched the kick high in the air. Another Torpedo tried to head it into the goal. She missed! The ball bounced toward the goal mouth. Bucky scooped it up and booted it far down the field to where Stookie, Jerry, and Lou were waiting. The attack was on!

Bucky hopped from foot to foot, watching and waiting. A roar rose up from the far end of the field. The 'Cats had scored!

Bucky did his best to hold on to their lead. Then, as the first half wound down, he missed a low kick to the left corner. He lay on his stomach in the dirt, listening to the cheers from the Torpedoes and the ref's whistle signaling the end of the first half.

A hand pulled him to his feet. "C'mon, Bucky, you can rest on the bench," Coach Bradley said with a smile.

Bucky gulped down some water and snacked on some juicy orange slices. When the second half began, he was refreshed and raring to go. But the coach put Jason in the goal. Bucky knew Coach Bradley always made sure everyone got to play every game. Still, it was hard to watch someone else take his position.

Jason had improved a lot since the start of the season. Even so, he was no match for the Torpedoes. Ten minutes into the half, they scored their second goal. Luckily, Lou put one past the Torpedoes' goalie a few minutes later to tie the game again.

Soon after, Bucky replaced Jason. Shot after shot barreled at him. Time and again he deflected high kicks, caught low rollers, and sent the ball toward the other end. Then, with the clock ticking off the last minutes of the game, he snagged the ball midchest. He scanned the field and spied Stookie at the center line. He booted the ball with all his might. It soared high into the air. Players from both teams rushed to get under it. But it was Stookie who controlled it. He was unstoppable, dodging around players to reach the goal.

Boom! The ball rocketed past the goalie, making the net billow with the force of Stookie's kick. The 'Cats took the lead!

The goal seemed to take the fight out of the Torpedoes. When the final whistle blew, the score read 'Cats 3, Torpedoes 2!

Coach Bradley was all smiles. His smile turned to surprise when Bucky pulled out the present and laid it in his hands.

"What's this?"

Bundy, the team captain, cleared his throat. "Coach Bradley, we just wanted to say thanks for being the best coach ever."

Then, just as Bucky had imagined it, the coach pulled the jacket out of the box and slipped it on. It fit perfectly. Bucky thought he saw tears in the coach's eyes when the coach saw the words stitched on the front.

"Thank you all," he said. "It's a wonderful present. You must have worked very hard to earn the money for it!"

Bucky and the others grinned at one another. Even Stookie was smiling.

"Now," the coach added, "everybody come to my house for ice cream!"

Coach

Bucky gathered up his belongings. Stookie was near him, doing the same.

"Hey, Stookie, can I try your computer game on the way to the coach's?" someone asked.

Stookie gave a shrug. "Sorry," he said. "I don't have it anymore." He caught Bucky's eye—and Bucky suddenly realized where Stookie had gotten the money to help pay for the jacket. He'd sold his computer game!

Bucky threw an arm around Stookie. "You sure know how to come through in the clutch," he said. "And I'm not just talking about that goal you made." As Stookie grinned, Bucky added, "Here's hoping the Soccer 'Cats stay together for the next season!"

SOCCER 'CATS

#1 The Captain Contest

#2 Operation Baby-Sitter

#3 Secret Weapon

#4 Hat Trick

#5 Master of Disaster

#6 Heads Up

#7 All Keyed Up

#8 You Lucky Dog

#9 Switch Play!

#10 Kick It!

#11 Making the Save